Pilgrim Thanksgiving

Pilgrim Thanksgiving

BY WILMA PITCHFORD HAYS

Illustrated by Leonard Weisgard

Coward-McCann, Inc.
New York

To my husband, who saw the need for this book

DAMARIS HOPKINS opened her eyes and sat up in bed, listening. Her heart beat hard, yet she did not know what had frightened her. The straw rustled under the blanket she slept on, but she was used to the rustly sound of straw. The wind whistled outside the split-log walls of her home. It whistled in the thatched roof close over her bed in the loft, but she was used to the sound of wind. The wind could not have frightened her.

Then Damaris remembered. This was the day the Indians would come. Governor Bradford had invited the Indians to come to a feast of thanksgiving.

"Our corn and other crops are gathered in," he had said. "We must give thanks to God because we have been able to grow enough food to feed us in the long winter ahead. And we must invite our neighbors, the Indians, to our thanksgiving feast. They gave us the seed of the corn to plant. And our Indian friend, Squanto, taught us how to plant it. Yes, they must be invited."

Governor Bradford had sent four men into the woods to hunt wild turkeys and ducks and deer for the feast. The holiday was to last three days.

Damaris knew that she should be happy. During the first hard winter, there had not been enough food or enough houses. The Pilgrims had been cold and hungry and sick. Many had died.

Now the summer sun and air had helped them grow strong and well again. They had eleven houses built. Many ears of colorful Indian corn hung in the Common House. There was enough food for everyone for the winter. Oh yes, there was much to be thankful for. But Damaris wished the Indians had not been invited to the thanksgiving feast.

She heard her older brother, Giles, turn in his straw bed nearby. He sat up, rubbing his eyes. Then he saw her.

"Why are you sitting there shivering?" Giles asked.

"Something waked me," Damaris said. "I thought it might be the Indians coming."

Giles laughed. "Are you still afraid of Indians?" he said. "The Indians are our friends —or Governor Bradford would not have invited them."

"Then why does Captain Standish continue to march the men up and down the hill? Why must Father and all the other men carry their muskets wherever they go?"

"Maybe because of wolves," Giles said.

Damaris shook her head. "It wasn't because of wolves that our friends who died were buried at night. It wasn't because of wolves that we planted corn over their graves early in the spring. I heard Father and Master Winslow talking. You know how brave Master Winslow is."

Giles nodded. Every boy in the colony hoped to grow up to be as brave as John Winslow.

"Master Winslow said we hid the graves so the Indians would not know that only half of us were left when the winter was over," Damaris said. "He says that many Indians fear us and would kill us if their chief, Massasoit, was not such a good honest friend."

"Well, Massasoit is good and the Indians are our friends now," Giles said. "And we had better get up and help with the work or they will be here before we are ready."

Giles jumped out of bed and pulled on breeches and jacket over the long underwear he had worn all night to help keep him warm. Then he went down the ladder of split logs nailed against the wall into the one room of the house.

Damaris heard her mother say, "Good morning, Giles." She could smell corn-meal porridge cooking for breakfast. She pushed her blankets back. She pulled on her long-sleeved waist. She stepped out of bed. She put on her long dark full skirt. She gave her yellow hair a quick pat and set her stiff white cap on her head. Then she went down the rough ladder.

Her mother was feeding porridge to little Oceanus, the baby brother who had been born on the *Mayflower*. He was a year old now. When he saw Damaris, he bounced up and down. He beat on his wooden dish with the pewter spoon Mother was helping him to use.

Damaris laughed. Oceanus was such a happy baby.

"Do you think he knows this is our first holiday in this new land?" Damaris asked Mother.

Mother smiled. "Maybe he feels how excited we all are," she said. "Now we must hurry. The sun is shining. It is going to be a beautiful day. We must finish the cooking."

"That's what we've been doing for days," Damaris said.

She hurried and ate her corn porridge. Then she watched the turkey roasting on the spit in the fireplace. Every few minutes she turned the iron hook that held the turkey over the hot coals. She wanted the turkey to be roasted evenly on all sides. If she didn't turn it, it would burn. The good roasting smell made Damaris so hungry she could hardly wait for the dinner.

The fire was hot on her face when she had to bend over it. She was glad when her mother said she could go now, and help the other children set the table outdoors. Not even the Common House was big enough to hold the guests for the feast. The men had built a long table of planks in the clearing away from the houses.

As Damaris carried a kettle of corn pudding out of the house, Master Goodman's little dog ran to meet her. He leaped up and barked. He licked her hand. She held the kettle higher.

"No, no, Little Dog," she said. "You must

wait, too. But I know how hungry you are."

When she had set the pot on the table, she knelt down. She patted the little dog's head and rubbed his ears. He made happy sounds. He jumped up to lick her cheek. She laughed.

Little Dog had come across the ocean on the *Mayflower* with Damaris. There had been only two dogs on the ship. Master Goodman's little spaniel was the smaller so she had always called him Little Dog.

Little Dog stayed close to her. He frisked about her feet so that she almost tripped over him as she carried dishes of food. But she laughed. He was such a loving, funny little dog, even if he wasn't very brave.

Little Dog was afraid of loud noises. He was afraid of the sound of the drums and trumpet when Captain Standish marched the men. He was afraid of thunder. He was afraid when the wolves howled in the woods.

The other children sometimes laughed at him when he put his tail between his legs and ran.

But Damaris knew what it was to be afraid. She petted the little dog. He liked to hide under her long full skirts. Oh yes, from there, he peeped out quite bravely.

Damaris was glad he liked to come to her. Every Sunday, as she listened to the long sermon in the cold meetinghouse, Little Dog crept under her wide skirts and kept her feet warm.

She went back and forth from the house with food. From the woods, came the sound of a trumpet, then a drum. *Rat-a-tat-tat! Rum-dee-dee-dum-dum-dum!*

Little Dog put his tail between his legs. He streaked for Damaris. She could feel him quivering against her ankles. She looked toward the woods. Her own heart beat faster. The Indians were coming.

Earlier that morning, Captain Standish and a group of Pilgrim men had gone to meet the Indians. Now, the drum sounds came nearer. *Rat-a-tat-tat! Rum-dee-dee-dum-dum-dum!*

Mothers came from the houses. Children ran to stand near the table. All looked toward the woods.

Captain Standish came from the woods first. He was not so tall as the other men, but he was straight and fearless. Behind him came a few Pilgrim men with muskets. Then came the Indians.

Their chief, Massasoit, led them. He was tall and walked proudly. Behind him came Indian men. Some of them carried wild turkey and deer meat for the feast.

The Indians wore leggings and a kind of shirt made of deerskin. Their hair was very black and long. It was cut off in front so that it would not hang in their eyes. Their faces were painted in a wide stripe from the forehead down to the chin. They carried bows and arrows and tomahawks.

They kept coming from the woods and coming from the woods. Damaris could not count fast enough to know how many there were. But she knew there were many more Indians than Pilgrims. There were only twenty white men and six growing boys left in all the Pilgrim village. There were a few women. More than half the Pilgrims were children. And all these Indians who came were tall, straight men.

Damaris heard her brother Giles counting softly. Then he said to his friend Richard Moore, who stood beside him, "I counted ninety."

"A few of their braves do not look much older than we are," Richard said.

"Perhaps they were allowed to come because they are good at the races and dances," Giles said.

"Father says the Indians will do some of their dances after the dinner. See that young brave with the wildcat tail around his neck. He is about my size. I will try to make friends with him."

Little Dog peeped from under Damaris' skirt. Damaris knelt down and patted his head.

"Don't you wish we were as brave as my brother Giles?" she said softly to the little dog. "But we're not. I know I will not sleep a wink all the time they are here. They look so silent and stern and fierce. And their tomahawks make me shiver."

Then the welcoming was over. The women and children hurried to put the food upon the long plank table. The men began to sit down on benches at the table. Chief Massasoit and Governor Bradford sat at the head. A few of the older Indian braves sat at the table with the Pilgrim men. Most of the Indians squatted on the ground.

Then the table was loaded with roast turkey and ducks. With clam stew and venison stew. With bread pudding and corn pudding. With

vegetables and a sweet cake made with dried
berries. The women and children sat down at the
table. Damaris sat next to her friend Remember.

They had worked so hard and the food smelled
so good that Damaris said, "I feel hollow clear to
my toes."

"Me, too," Remember said. "But we'll have to
wait for the prayers, you know."

Damaris reached out to take a crumb of meat that had fallen when a plump turkey was pushed off the spit.

"Sh-h-h," her brother Giles said, looking across the table. "Elder Brewster is ready to give thanks."

Damaris lowered her head quickly. For a long time she kept her eyes almost closed. How good everything smelled. How long Elder Brewster prayed. Damaris felt her stomach groan. She was so hungry.

Then across from her she saw Richard Moore. His head was bowed. His hands were folded properly. There was a thankful look on his face. Damaris knew that Richard was an orphan who lived with Elder Brewster and helped with the work in return for his living. His two sisters and his little brother had died in the sickness of the first long winter. Yet he was grateful, now, for food and good crops and friends.

Damaris bowed her head again and said inside herself, "Thank Thee, dear God, for my good mother and father, for my brother Giles and my sister Constance and baby Oceanus—for everything."

She felt a little stir under her skirt. A warm furry body pressed against her ankles.

"And thank Thee, too, for Little Dog and his funny ways that make us laugh," she added.

After Elder Brewster sat down, Governor Bradford prayed. Damaris saw how politely the In-

dians listened. How quiet they were although they could not understand a word. They seemed to know that this was the white man's way of saying thank you to the Great Father who takes care of all people, red and white.

After the prayers, everyone began to eat. They ate and ate and ate. Damaris kept putting scraps of skin and meat on the ground behind her for Little Dog. Several times she left the table to help the other girls and the women bring more food. They passed food to the Indians squatting on the ground, too. But Damaris always managed to work at the table. She did not want to walk among the Indians.

After a while she saw her brother Giles stand up and go over to the young Indian with the wild-cat tail around his neck.

Giles smiled at the young brave and squatted down beside him.

Damaris saw that the young Indian was looking at the hunting knife stuck in Giles' belt. Giles was very proud of the sharp knife. His father had

given it to him for his birthday. When he saw the Indian look at it, Giles took the knife from his belt and let the Indian take it. The young Indian turned it over and over. He held up a coarse hair from the wildcat tail and touched the knife to it. The hair split in two. The young brave smiled. He touched the sharp knife with his finger. Damaris saw his dark eyes shine as he put one hand over the knife to show how much he liked it.

"Take it," Giles said. "It is a present. Take it."

The young Indian could not understand the words. He held the knife against his heart. He seemed to say, "Is it mine? Do you mean to give it?"

Giles nodded. "Yes. Take it. It is a present from me to you."

Damaris could hardly believe her ears. Giles had an old knife but this knife was his best one. He liked it better than anything else he had. Yet he had given it to the Indian boy.

Giles had said he wanted to be a friend to the

Indian boy and he meant what he said. Giles had given his best.

Damaris saw the joy that came over the Indian boy's face. He held the knife close in his hand, and looked and looked at it. Then he reached down and picked up his tomahawk. He handed it to Giles. Giles took the tomahawk gravely. The Indian boy made signs that Giles was to keep it.

Damaris heard Giles say, "Thank you."

Why, they are like any two boys giving each other presents, she thought in surprise.

At last even the hungriest Indian and Pilgrim was full. It was time for the hymns and dances and speeches. Bonfires were lighted for warmth and to give light as the early night came on. The Pilgrims and Indians drew near the fires. The Pilgrims sang hymns. The Indians chanted the songs of their people.

Then Captain Standish gave a parade. He marched his men up the one street past the houses to the cannon on the hill. The trumpet and the drum led the way. *Rat-a-tat-tat! Rum-dee-dee-dum-dum-dum!* The men marched back again. The Indians sat and watched.

When Captain Standish and his men sat down, some of the Indians stood up. Dusk was coming now. The forest stood like a black wall around the little clearing. Damaris thought the Indians seemed very tall in the firelight.

They made a circle. They hunched forward.

They began to dance. High leaps. Strange yells. Raising their tomahawks high.

Damaris felt her heart beat hard in her throat. She saw her brother Giles standing near the bonfire. She slipped through the circle of people and stood close to her big brother. Maybe Giles knew she was trembling, because he took her hand.

"Do not be afraid, little sister," he said. "The Indians dance about the things they do in their daily living. They act out everything they do. They have a dance of planting corn. A dance of hunting. This is their war dance. They show it to us as Captain Standish showed them our men marching. Watch. Their ways are interesting."

At that moment the Indians let out a great yell and swung their tomahawks high. Damaris felt a swish of her skirts. Little Dog was cuddling against her ankles. She looked down and saw his two bright eyes peeping out at her. She had to laugh.

"It is only a dance, Little Dog," she said to him.

But she held on to her brother's hand.

"Giles," she said. "The Indians are going to stay three days. Where will they sleep tonight?"

"Massasoit and some of the older braves will be guests in our houses. But most of them will sleep outside on the ground. Father says they are used to sleeping that way."

"Will we have Indians in our house?" Damaris asked.

"Of course," Giles said.

"Now I know I won't sleep a wink," she said.

The war dance ended and the braves sat down. Another group of Indians stood up. Damaris watched them swing their arms as they bent over the earth. They bent and rose. They bent to the ground again. She watched them, puzzled. What did this dance mean? They seemed to be picking something up and putting it down again.

She saw them hold out their hands. They wiggled their fingers. They stamped upon the ground. And suddenly Damaris knew. This must be the dance of the planting of the corn.

How well she remembered Squanto teaching her and all the other Pilgrims how to dig holes in the earth. Then take a herring fish from the basketful they had caught in the brook. Three herring in a hill. Herring heads meeting in the center. A little soil pushed over them with the toe, then several kernels of Indian corn dropped in. More soil pushed over the corn. The soil stamped down with their feet.

This was the way the Indians had always planted corn, Squanto had said. And this was the way the braves were dancing now.

Damaris saw the Indians lift their hands and look toward the forest and make loud noises. This was to frighten off the wolves.

She knew. She had done everything they were doing in their dance.

There had been so few Pilgrims to do all the work of planting and building, that even the smallest child had worked. Damaris had planted corn. She had taken turns with other children to guard the cornfields from the wolves. The children had guarded by day. The men guarded by night. They kept the wolves from digging up the herring and ruining the corn.

Damaris looked at the Common House. There the ripe ears of corn were drying. She had even helped to pick the corn and hang it there. She was proud that she had helped to raise the corn which they would eat.

At the end of the corn dance, each Indian tossed a handful of corn upon hot stones beside the fire. The corn began to hop and jump about on the hot stones. Then–*pop, pop, pop*. Kernels of corn leaped into the air. They popped open. They were like large white snowflakes flying through the air.

One fell at Damaris' feet. She picked it up. She put it in her mouth. She knew it was good to eat. Squanto had shown the children this kind of corn which would pop open when it was hot. Pop-corn.

Another kernel fell near her. Little Dog came

out from under her skirts and sniffed at it. Damaris took up the white kernel. She let Little Dog eat it from her fingers.

He frisked happily at her feet.

"You like pop-corn," she said. "It is a gift from the Indians."

Thoughtfully she looked at the Indians. The dancers had gone back to sit in the circle now. Their faces were all turned upward to look at Governor Bradford. Governor Bradford was standing to make a good-night speech. He was young and tall and wise.

The Indians listened politely. Their pipes glowed as they smoked and watched this young white chief with the kind voice. Later, Squanto would tell them all he said. Squanto could speak both English and Indian. Now the Indians were full of good food. They were warm before the fire. They liked to listen to Governor Bradford's voice.

"We are your friends," he said. "And you are our friends."

Damaris saw the Indians nod as if they understood that he liked them.

Why, she thought, they want to be friends. In their dances, they have tried to show us what their life is like. Now they are trying to understand us. She listened to Governor Bradford.

"Some other white men have not treated you well," he said to the Indians. "Some white men came to this land and stole your furs and went away.

"We will not leave. It has been hard to grow enough food to keep us alive, but we have done it. You helped us learn how. We have built homes."

He pointed to the one row of plank houses with low roofs of straw and thatch and grass.

"We trade with you. We give you knives and the pretty beads and earrings you like. We give you iron cooking pots. You pay us with furs you trap in the woods.

"Do not fear that we will leave to go back over

the ocean, no matter how hard it is to live in this wild land. We are not easily discouraged.

"We love freedom. We came here to be free. We came to worship God as we believed to be right.

"God has given us crops. He has made you our friends. We will stay and make this new world our home."

Governor Bradford sat down. There was a murmuring among the Indians. Some nodded their heads. They seemed to say, "This white man speaks true words. His heart is good. He is honest. We can trust him. Let us all be friends as he has said."

Damaris saw her father stand up. Other fathers and mothers stood. It was time to go to bed.

Damaris and Giles walked together. Little Dog trotted at their heels. When they came to Master Goodman's house, they left Little Dog.

"Rest well, Little Dog," Damaris said. "Tomorrow will be another feast day. And the day after that, too. Perhaps we shall do this every year when the crops are in."

Later, when she and Giles were in their straw beds in the loft of their home, Giles said, "What a wonderful day. Did you ever have so much fun?"

For a moment Damaris did not answer. She was thinking. It had been fun. So much good food all at one time. The friendly dances of the Indians. The pride and happiness in knowing that the Common House was full of corn that she had helped to raise. The peace and trust she felt in her heart as she listened to a good man like Governor Bradford.

Damaris was happy. And she was no longer afraid.

"Giles," she said softly. "You cannot be afraid of people who have feasted with you. You feel friends with people who have brought food to share with you and have eaten yours."

"Ho," he said. "How different you talk. You

were not going to sleep a wink tonight. Remember?"

He was teasing. But Damaris did not care. It was good teasing. She knew her brother was glad that this had been a happy day of thanksgiving for her, too.

So much to be thankful for—a home, food, loving father and mother and sister and brothers. For freedom and God's care. And Damaris was thankful that today she had learned to be real friends with their neighbors, the Indians.

The people in this story were real, Damaris and Giles, even Little Dog.

I visited Plymouth where the Pilgrims lived. I saw the tall trees and wondered how the Pilgrim children felt that first Thanksgiving Day, when they watched the painted Indian braves come from the forest. What really happened?

Later I read what was written by two of the great men who were there that day, Governor Bradford and Master Winslow. Then I wrote this book so you could know what happened.